D1599945

CAN MAN

KILLER OF COP-KILLERS

BOOK FOUR

A NOVELLA BY JOHN DITTO

ISBN: 978-1-7343501-1-1
email: canman@reagan.com
website: canmanspub.com

Acknowledgments

Thanks to my sister, Denise Ditto Satterfield, Author of *The Tooth Collector Fairies Series www. toothcollectorfairies.com. I could not have done it without you.*

Lilia Fabry created and updates my website for me. Canmanspub.com. I thank her so much for all of her help. I highly recommend her if you need a website. Freelancewriterdesign.com

Thanks to Marvin D. Cloud who does a wonderful job of formatting my manuscript into book form and taking my original art and turning it into a book cover. For more information, visit www. marvindcloud.com.

Introduction

The Can Man finds himself dealing with a cop killer who turns the tables on him. Not only is the Can Man being hunted, but the cop killer also has lots of friends with him.

Chapter One

It's another Monday morning, Jack thought as he looked up at his slow turning ceiling fan. He knew he had about an hour to get to his pub and open up for his daytime regulars. He liked to lay in bed for a little bit and think about things he wanted to do, and things he needed to do. He thought about all he had done as the Can Man. He asked himself a big question. Was he just a vigilante? That really bothered him. Was he? He presented himself with a scenario. He's was walking down the street. He sees a police officer being overpowered and in mortal danger. He runs over and puts the attacker in a chokehold until the officer is freed and able to put the cuffs on the suspect. The suspect subsequently dies. Jack would probably get a citizens award from the police department and a key to the city from the mayor. The last thing anyone would call him would be a vigilante. Jack decided that what he was doing was no different. He wanted no awards, recognition or a key to the city.

Jack jumped out of bed, did some sit up's, and push-ups before taking a hot shower. Getting dressed he felt pretty good. It was a beautiful morning so he decided to walk the few blocks to his pub. It would be a great way to start his day. He left his apartment and thought about going one block over to the small local supermarket and pick up an apple and a bottle of mineral water. They always had the best produce.

As he turned the corner he heard screaming and yelling. A big scuffle was going on right outside the supermarket. Jack couldn't see anything because of the parked cars along the curb. The loud noises did not stop. Running across the street in between two parked cars, Jack saw a terrible situation. A very large homeless looking man was on top of what appeared to be a police officer. Jack thought *this is crazy*. He was just thinking about this same scenario this morning. There was no time to lose. He ran over and leaned on the back of the suspect. He reached under his neck and started applying a chokehold. The guy was surprised but it was too late for him to react. Jack kept the pressure on until the guy let go and was going limp. He eased back a bit and pulled the suspect to one side. To Jack's shock Firella was the police officer under the homeless man.

She immediately rolled the guy over on his stomach, and put the cuffs on him.

Now that the situation was under control Jack thought, *here comes my hug*.

Instead Firella shouted, "Stay out of police matters, Jack. We can handle ourselves." She pulled out her radio and called for a unit to pick up the creep.

Jack was dumbfounded. He'd never seen that look on Firella's face before.

"Sorry," he said. "I didn't mean to interfere with police business."

Jack walked into the supermarket and headed towards the produce section. He wasn't in a big hurry to go back outside. He didn't want to get snapped at again. When he finally left the store the suspect had already been picked up and Firella was gone.

Walking the rest of the way to his pub he kept running everything through his mind. *What the heck did I do wrong?*

Later after the last of the daytime regulars left, Jack was alone and wiping down the bar thinking what a crazy day he'd had so far. That's when he heard the little bell ring above the door. Looking up, he saw two small, but rough looking men with lots of tattoos, even on their faces, enter the pub. They quickly ran over to Jack with large knives.

Jack thought, *this can't be happening. Don't these idiots know this is a cop hang out?*

The smaller of the two yelled with a heavy Hispanic accent, "Give us all your money! Pronto!"

Jack turned to the register and hit the open button. He did have a pistol in a drawer but it was too far from the register. As Jack was gathering the cash he looked up at the mirror and behind the suspects he could see a police car waiting for the light to change. When Jack turned back around he tossed the money so that some of it fell off the bar and scattered on the floor.

The bigger one said, "Are you trying to be funny?"

Jack said, "No. No. I'm just nervous." He raised his hands high over his head. While they were picking up bills everywhere, Jack kept his eyes on the police car. *Come on, look this way*, he thought. The light turned green and the police car started to move forward.

Jack's heart sank. Then for some unknown reason the policeman glanced over to the pub. Now Jack wasn't sure if the policeman saw what was going on. Was there a glare on the window preventing him to see the robbery in progress? With the patrol car gone, Jack turned his attention back to the two street thugs. They had all the cash picked up and Jack thought, *good, now get out.*

The smaller one said, "Where is the rest?"

Jack responded, "That's it. I've only been open for a short while today." Then came the question Jack didn't want to hear.

"Where is the safe? You take us to the back where the safe is."

Jack knew that this could be real bad. Once they get you behind closed doors, they can do anything they want, including stabbing him. With no weapon on him, he could find himself trying to fight off the two street thugs with just his hands. The only thing he could think of was to try and talk them out of going to the back.

"Listen guys, that's it. I have no more money in the back."

The smaller one said, "Take us now or we will cut you up bad."

Jack was quickly running out of ideas. The last thing he wanted was to be kneeling down in front of his safe putting in the combination with his back to these guys with their knives.

Like an answer from heaven, through the windows Jack saw the most beautiful site. From both sides of the pub were numerous police officers approaching the front door with pistols drawn. Jack had his poker face on and didn't want to alert the thieves that they were about to be nabbed.

The larger of the two then stuck his knife close to Jack's face and said, "I'm going to stick this in your face if you don't take us to your safe!"

Looking over the guys shoulder, Jack could see that the police were at the door.

Jack turned his attention back to the thug and said, "I don't think so," and he immediately took one step backwards.

The thug was moving his long knife forward towards Jack while yelling in Spanish when the little metal bell above the door rang loudly almost causing it to fly off its frame. Five officers rushed in with their pistols drawn. Officer Martinez was shouting in Spanish for them to drop their knives and get on the floor. They immediately complied. The two street thugs had no chance and were swarmed by the police and handcuffed. As they were being frisked down, Jack caught his breath and started thanking the guys for getting there in the nick of time.

Officer Jesse Martinez said, "That was me that spotted what was going on here in here from my car."

Jack responded, "Oh, Okay. I was afraid you didn't see. But just in case you did I raise my hands up so you could see there was a robbery going on."

Jesse answered, "I'm glad you did that. That's how I knew you were in trouble."

They shook hands. That's when Jack noticed that Firella and Sasha were part of the arresting team. After Jack's encounter with Firella that morning, he wasn't sure if she was still mad at him.

Firella walked over to Jack and asked, "Can I talk to you for a moment over here?" She led him to the end of the bar. "Jack, I want to apologize for my behavior this morning. You helped me when I really needed it and I snapped at you instead of thanking you."

Jack said, "I was just trying to help you."

Firella said, "You did and I thank you so much. But the reason I snapped at you was because I let that guy surprise me from behind. He got the upper hand on the situation. In the Academy they teach us that you can never ever let that happen. You know, I'm new to the department. The last thing I want Chief Mike to think is that I can't handle myself on the street. I was mad at myself, not you. And I am sorry I took it out on you."

Jack responded, "Thanks Firella. Glad I could help."

She said, "I'll come back tonight and we can talk some more."

Firella and Sasha were the last two officers to leave.

Jack thought to himself, *this has been one heck of a roller coaster ride today. And I'm really glad Firella isn't mad at me anymore.*

Chapter Two

At 5 o'clock Chief Mike and Officer Martinez walked in and sat at the bar. Jack filled two mugs from the beer tap and walked over.

Chief Mike spoke first. "Jack are you doing okay after what happened here earlier?"

"Yes, I'm good. Thanks for asking," Jack said. "So you have those two locked up?"

Chief Mike said, "Oh yeah. They aren't going anywhere for a while."

Officer Martinez said, "Jack, remember that street gang that killed that meter reader? They had a leader that called himself Lobo?"

Jack said, "Of course I remember. That poor girl ran into here after being attacked by them. They grabbed her from under the over pass down by the bayou."

Martinez said, "Well, those two today were members of that gang."

Jack took a step back. "That could've been a lot worse."

Chief Mike said, "They told us that their leader Lobo was missing and that their gang was breaking up. They were the only two left."

Jack said, "Well that's good. I'm glad that gang is no longer here."

Chief Mike said, "Jack. They told us that Lobo used to come in here for a beer about once a week. Did you know that?"

Jack tried his best to look surprised. "Of course not. I had no idea that he came in here or why he came in here. Lots of other bars around. Mine is full of off-duty police."

The chief said, "Lobo came in here because it was full of police. He did it to show his gang how brave he was."

Jack said, "I wish I had known what he looked like. I would have pointed him out to you guys."

"Well, don't feel bad Jack," the chief responded. "You can imagine how all of us felt after learning he was right in the middle of us and we didn't know it."

Jack said, "Well, it all ended safely."

The chief said, "If Officer Martinez here hadn't seen your raised hands this afternoon, it wouldn't have ended safely.

Jack asked, "What are you mean?"

Martinez said, "They thought maybe you knew what happened to Lobo. They were going to take you in back and cut you up to make you talk."

Jack was a little shaken to hear that. He wanted to bring this conversation to a close. He said, "They could've killed me for nothing because I didn't know their leader."

Jack told the officers he had to get back to work.

Later that evening the bell rang above the door. Jack looked up to see Firella walking in. He could feel himself becoming smitten with her. And maybe, just maybe she felt that way about him. It took all of Jack's power to try and not look overly excited to see her. But he was excited and could not stop his great big smile. Walking over to where she sat at the bar, Jack spoke first.

"I'm so glad to see you. What a day you've had."

Firella answered, "What a day we both had! You especially. After pulling that crazy guy off of me. And instead of thanking you, I bite your head off. Then you get held up by two street thugs. Geez, Jack. Maybe you should've just stayed in bed."

Jack said, "No. No. That's not me. I was glad I was there for you this morning. I should be thanking you and your fellow officers for arresting those two thugs today."

"Of course Jack, that's what we do," Firella said. "I think there is something else you should know." She had Jack's attention. "The homeless guy that jumped me this morning is the same guy that mugged Jolene in your parking lot," Firella said.

Jack said, "Are you kidding me? I thought that guy would've been locked up. What happened? How did he get out?"

Firella explained. "The judge decided he should've been in a mental hospital instead of jail. After a short stint there they released him because of overcrowding."

"Oh that's great," Jack said sarcastically. "And what does he do? Goes right back to attacking women."

Firella nodded in agreement. She said, "I was wondering, can I get a beer?"

Jack felt stupid. "I'm sorry. I just got caught up in our conversation."

Firella laughed. "No problem. I was caught up in it, too." She took a sip of beer. "There was a big difference between Jolene's attack and mine."

Jack asked, "How so?"

"He was mugging Jolene for her purse. He just wanted her money. But with me, he wasn't after my money. He was after me. He told Sergeant Taylor he was trying to kill me. He somehow thinks all of his problems are because of the police."

Jack said, "Oh, I see. It wasn't you personally. It was the police in general and you were wearing your uniform. Your attack was on all police."

Firella said, "Correct. And you know what? He has got all of our attention." Firella took another sip of her beer.

Jack said, "Well, I hope he is locked up for a very long time."

Firella licked the suds from her upper lip and said, "Me too!"

Jack asked, "By the way. What's his name?"

"Well you're not going to believe this but his name is James 'Yellow Feather' O'Keefe."

Jack said, "Oh c'mon Firella. How can a big guy like that with dirty blonde hair possibly think he is an Indian?"

Firella nodded in agreement. "I know, I know. But he thinks he's part Indian because his grandpa told him that when he was a boy. Then as an adult, he went and got his name changed to officially include 'Yellow Feather'. Some of us just referred to him as 'Dirty Feather' for short."

Jack said, "Oh, I don't care what he's called. I just hope the Judge locks him up for real this time.

"Me too," Firella said. She took the last sip of her beer and said, "Okay, Jack, I'm ready for my free second beer."

"No, no, these are all on me. You and your fellow officers probably saved my life this afternoon."

Firella said, "But Jack. You're going to go out of business if you don't charge us."

"Don't worry," Jack said. "I'm fine with all of my regular customers."

Firella held out her empty mug and said, "OK, fill her up!"

Chapter Three

Jack decided to take the night off on his Can Man duties and stay at home. He'd had a pretty big day. Sitting at his small kitchen table he thought about something Firella told him earlier. She said her attacker, Dirty Feather, was trying to kill her because she was a cop. If Jack hadn't intervened, Dirty Feather might have succeeded in choking her to death. Does that make Dirty Feather a cop killer? Would he have stopped just shy of killing her? Or would he have really killed her? Jack posed another bigger question to himself. Should the Can Man kill someone who hasn't killed a cop but thinks they would? *Waiting until a police officer has been slain is not an option*, he thought to himself. *I'm not about to stand aside for that to happen.*

Thinking back a few years ago Jack remembered when he had his knife under Ray Ray's throat. Instead of killing him, he let Officer Garza arrest him. Before that when Officer Morgan was about to get his skull crushed, the Can Man ended that threat. Thinking through all of these events and more, Jack came to the conclusion that there is no clear-cut answer. He thought, if the Can Man believes that an officer is in mortal danger, the Can Man will end the threat. This seemed to be the answer. Jack was now ready to go get some sleep.

The next morning it was another beautiful day. Jack thought again about walking to work, stopping by the local market and getting an apple. Yesterday's events flashed through his mind. He thought, *maybe I shouldn't risk it.* Snapping at himself he thought, *wait just a minute now. Wouldn't that be letting the bad guys win? I refuse to do that. I'm going to go where I want, when I want. Besides those two gangbangers are in jail along with Dirty Feather.*

That afternoon at the County Courthouse, the two attempted robbery suspects appeared before Judge Dinkle. He was known as a lenient judge that took it easy on defendants. Prosecutors didn't like him but defense attorneys did. However, he wasn't about to release these two back into the community to rob and attack people again. He told them through an interpreter that they both had been deported three times. He went on to say, "I don't even want you here in our overcrowded jails" Banging down his gavel twice he said to his bailiff, "Turn these two over to the feds."

The robbery suspects yelled something in Spanish and were escorted out.

Firella and Jack we're both sitting in the back of the court room when the bailiff brought out Dirty Feather. He looked mad that he was there.

Judge Dinkle didn't really care if he was mad or not. He looked at him and said, "What are you doing back here again? They told me that you were much better. That you weren't hearing voices in your head anymore."

Dirty Feather glared at the judge.

Dinkle went on. "If I send you to prison you will for sure not get any better. In my opinion you need to be in a mental institution where they can take better care of you."

Dirty Feather replied in a loud voice, "If you send me back there, you will regret it. I promise."

The Judge leaned forward and asked, "Would you rather go to prison for 30 months or to the institution till they say you're well?"

Dirty Feather answered, "Neither. Let me go."

Dinkle smiled and said, "That isn't going to happen. The court sentences you to go back to the institution for care and evaluation."

And with that he slammed his gavel down and said to his bailiff, "Next case."

Leaving the court room, Dirty Feather was tussling with the deputies. But it was useless. They were as big as he was and there were four of them.

Jack turned to Firella and said, "That guy is really bad news. And to think he was on top of you trying to strangle you is a very frightful scenario."

"Yeah I know," Firella answered. "I just wish Dinkle would have put him in prison for a long time. Now he can get out whenever some doctor says he's not a threat to society."

Jack said, "Well, let's hope he they keep him for a long time."

Firella nodded in agreement as they exited the courthouse. Standing on the steps she stopped and turned around to Jack and said, "Seeing Dirty Feather again brought back all those bad memories of that day. And I want you to know that the only good thing that happened that day was you." She hugged Jack.

Jack said, "I'm just glad I happened along to be there for you."

Still hugging Jack she said, "I just hope you happen along some more."

Jack gave a little chuckle and said, "I'll see what I can do."

Firella waved goodbye. "I need to get back to the station. Sasha is waiting for me in the car. The Chief wants us to go work radar at a school zone."

Jack answered, "Okay. I'm heading back to Suzanna's. Jolene came in to cover for me so I need to get back."

Chapter Four

Jack walked into the pub. Jolene was closing out the tabs of the last few of his daytime regulars. Big Don turned to Jack on his way out and said, "We like her better than you. She is a lot cuter!"

Jack responded, "I can't argue with you there." After they left it was just Jolene and Jack. She turned to Jack, "How did it go at the courthouse? Please tell me they locked up that maniac."

Jack answered, "Well not exactly. Judge Dinkle sent him back to the mental hospital."

"For how long?" Jolene asked.

"Till they think he is well," he said.

Jolene sat down at an empty table. "Well that's not very comforting."

Jack said, "Yeah I know. Firella, of course wanted him locked up too. You both have been attacked by that lunatic."

Jolene said a curious thing. "I wish someone could do something about him."

Jack decided not to respond to that one.

He asked Jolene, "Do you want to go home now or just stay?"

She said, "I will just stay since I'm already here. As a matter fact, you can takeoff if you want to Jack. I got this."

After thinking about her offer for about one and a half seconds Jack responded, "Thanks Jolene. I think I'm going to take you up on your offer." He picked up his keys off the bar and said, "Call me if you need me."

Jack wasn't used to having days off so this was a pleasant break. He usually takes Sundays off and Jolene takes care of Suzanna's. Being off in the middle of the week was nice. He found himself thinking about Firella. He wished he could hang out with her but she's busy working the school zone with Sasha. Laughing to himself he thought, *I guess I could speed through the school zone and while she's writing my ticket I could talk to her. Bad idea.* His thoughts then drifted to the Can Man. He thought, *it's still daylight so no Can Man activities right now. However, late tonight sounds good.*

Getting home he turned on his TV that he never watched and laid down on the couch. When he woke up it was already dark outside. It was almost 10 o'clock. He called the pub and Jolene said she was getting ready to lock up and there was no problems. Jack thanked her for letting him have an unscheduled day off.

Jolene said, "No problem. Have a fun night."

He said okay not really knowing what she was talking about.

Online Jack found some heavy socks with plastic pads on the soles to help prevent slips while wearing. He thought they might be better for tightrope walking instead of those rubber booties. They had been delivered and Jack was thinking tonight would be a good night to try them out. They wouldn't be good to wear if it was raining but all the other nights should be okay.

He ordered some Chinese food for delivery. He decided to eat before putting on his Can Man disguise and make his rounds to check on police officers walking their beats. While eating Jack was thinking how everything was getting better. Dirty Feathers was locked up in the mental hospital and the last two of Lobos gangbangers were gone. And he and Firella were getting along again. He looked at his watch and it was just past 11 o'clock. Putting on his hat, poncho and new footwear he turned off his lights and quietly headed out for the evening. This was the kind of night Jack liked. Clear, cloudless, and lots of stars. The starlight aided his night vision binoculars.

Jack spent the next few hours tight roping from building to building checking on officers walking their beats. He was on the building across the street from his local supermarket and was thinking how much he liked his new footwear. Looking at his watch he decided to head back to his apartment.

Jack quietly walked about halfway across the roof top heading for the tight rope that lead to his apartment. He spotted something. He froze in place and carefully pulled out his night vision binoculars. Raising them slowly he zoomed in on the object. It was the worst thing that he could imagine. Standing between him and his tight rope back home was none other than Jolene. He could feel his heart pounding. His mind raced with questions. Should he flee or stay. And what on earth is she doing up here? Still standing there frozen, Jolene started walking towards him.

"Hi Jack. Out for a walk on rooftops?"

Chapter 5

All Jack could think was, this is bad, really bad.

"Don't worry Jack. Your secret is safe with me," Jolene assured him. "I figured out a long time ago that you were the Can Man."

Jack remained frozen, not moving a muscle. He continued to think through all of his options. Denial didn't seem to be one of them.

Jolene made a good suggestion. "C'mon Jack, let's go over to your apartment."

Jack decided to accept his situation and speak.

"OK. Just go down to the fire escape and come over to my building."

Jolene responded, "That won't be necessary. You're not the only one who can tight rope."

Jack looked at her. "I'm impressed. I'll go first."

Climbing down the fire escape Jack looked up in the night sky to see the dim view of Jolene tight roping over to his rooftop, then climbing down to his fire escape.

He complemented her. "Not bad."

She responded," I've been a gymnast my whole life. Let's go inside."

Entering his living room through the window Jack said, "Make yourself at home. The kitchen is in through there. I'm going into my bedroom to take all of this off."

Jolene went into the kitchen cabinet and grabbed two glasses. She filled them with ice and made two scotch and waters. She figured Jack needed a drink too.

She yelled from the living room, "I made you a drink Jack."

Jack yelled back, "Great. I think we both need one. I'm going to take a quick shower. I'll be out shortly."

Jolene took a sip of her drink and looked around at Jack's apartment. It was her first time there and she was a little curious to see how he lived. There was nothing fancy about his place. No big TV or anything that might look like a man cave. It was a little on the sparse side and could use a woman's touch.

She could tell that Jack's life was really at the Pub. All the people, TVs and camaraderie. That's where his life was. Not here. This was just a place where he slept. Jolene heard the shower stop.

Sitting on his small couch she waited for him to come out of his bedroom. The door opened and there stood Jack in his bathrobe.

He didn't say anything. Walking over to his table he pulled out a wooden chair and sat down.

Jolene asked, "Are you all right?"

Looking up at her Jack said, "What do you think? I knew this couldn't last forever. But I guess it's over now."

Jolene stood up and walked over to Jack and put her hand on his slumped shoulder. She said, "Jack it's not over unless you wanted to be over."

Raising his head to look at her he asked, "You are OK with what I do?"

Walking back over to the couch she answered, "I don't know what I am. I could argue either side of it if it's right or wrong. But know this. I have no intentions of stopping you or reporting you. As you know I'm dating Officer Alford and it gives me some comfort knowing you are out there for them. You don't have to say anything but when my friend Maria was found on that rooftop with her sniper rifle, I had mixed feelings. After some time passed I realized she wasn't the person I thought she was. Jack, no one ever gets to thank you. I thank you for saving Chief Dickens life. I thank you for saving other cops lives that I don't know about. And I don't want to know. But I do want you to know that I am okay with it and I understand why you do it."

Jack stood up and held his hands out and said, "So you are okay with this?"

Jolene immediately said, "Yes."

Jack started pacing back-and-forth.

"I gotta to be honest. This is not at all how I thought it was going to go."

Jolene walked over to the table and sat down.

"Many things happened, big and small, that led me to figure out that you were the Can Man. I'm not going to name them all. But if I can figure it out, so could a detective."

Jack said, "You are right. Chief Mike has already let me know that the Can Man and I have some similarities. Like we both came on the scene at about the same time."

They were both sitting opposite of each other at the small wooden table. Jolene then asked, "I'm guessing you try to ease drop on policeman conversations at the bar to try to pick up info?"

Jack looked at her and said, "Yes that's right. That's the only place I can pick it up."

Jolene leaned back in her chair and asked, "I bet you wish you could listen to their conversations out at the tables?"

Jack started to speak but Jolene continued. "Even better. I bet you wish you could just ask them for info on someone who is a suspected cop killer."

She now let Jack respond. "Of course I do, but I can't be ease dropping at tables. And just come out and ask for an update on a suspect."

Jolene stood up and leaned forward and said, "But I can."

Jack's knee-jerk response was, "No, no, no. I refuse to let you get involved in this. It is very, very dangerous. You could go to prison for a very long time for helping me. It's called aiding and abetting."

"Yes, I know," Jolene answered. "Jack if I hear something at the tables or from Alfie and I tell you, there is nothing you can do. You didn't ask me anything. It's just me making conversation, right?"

Jack answered, "It sounds like you have given this a lot of thought."

"I have," she answered. It's late and I'm ready to go home."

Jack also stood up and said, "Let me walk you downstairs."

Jolene headed towards his open window and with 1 foot outside she said, "Actually I'm going to use your tight ropes to get back. My car is only two blocks over." She ducked out the rest of the way and was gone.

Jack shut the window and said to himself, *well this is an interesting development I didn't see coming.* He turned out the lights and went to bed.

Chapter 6

"James Yellow Feather O'Keefe," the doctor said reading from a clipboard. "It says that you were here before and then released because the institution thought you were better. So what did you do? You went out and tried to strangle a female cop. Is that about right?"

O'Keefe knew that if he wanted to get released again, that he was going to have to fool them by pretending to be getting better. "Yes that's true. I haven't been feeling well and I overreacted and I am terribly sorry."

The doctor responded back, "Overreacted? You almost killed that lady cop."

O'Keefe looked down and said, "I am so sorry I did that. And I'm glad I'm here so I can get better."

The doctor handed the nurse his clipboard and said, "Well, we are glad that you feel that way and we want you to get better, too. I'm going to administer you a round of shock treatment. Because the truth is you could just be saying what you think we want to hear. This treatment will make sure that you are grounded."

O'Keefe immediately responded, "Oh, that won't be necessary. I'm feeling much more grounded now."

Two big white coated orderlies came into the room. One was pushing a cart with a metal box on top and a few gauges and some wires on the side. The nurse took the electrical cord and walked over to a wall outlet and plugged it in.

O'Keefe kept saying, "This is not necessary, I feel just fine and grounded."

No one paid him any attention to him. The doctor placed a heavy rubber teeth guard in O'Keefe's mouth and said, "Bite down and hold this there." He went back to the cart and put on some very thick rubber gloves. Picking up the two metal rod objects with wires attached he turned around and said, "Everyone back."

O'Keefe was truly terrified. Beads of sweat were running down his face. His hands and feet were secured to the railing on his bed.

Leaning over O'Keefe the doctor placed a metal rod on each side of O'Keefe's head. He said to his nurse, "Two, four second intervals at 20% and James Yellow Feather O'Keefe, this first one is courtesy of Judge Dinkle. Okay nurse, we're ready."

And with that she flipped a switch and O'Keefe stiffened. Then stiffened again as the second current went through his skull.

The doctor removed the rods and handed them back to the nurse. He said, "Mr. O'Keefe are you still with us?"

Groggily but conscious, O'Keefe slurred, "I'm still with you and grounded."

The doctor replied, "Well that's good. I will come back tomorrow and check on you again." Turning around he said, "Nurse, gentlemen, let's leave Mr. O'Keefe alone so he can get some rest."

Nurse Bonnet shut O'Keefe's door. She turn to ask the doctor a question. Dr. Wong looked at his nurse and asked, "Yes Miss Bonnet, Do you have a question?"

Walking together down the hall she asked, "Doctor, he seems so sincere when he talks to you. It sounds like he's getting better. Do you think O'Keefe is getting better?"

Dr. Wong replied, "Well Nurse Bonnet, it's hard to tell. Patients will often say what they think you want to hear. So even though it seems like what I'm doing is cruel, it is necessary. We are just trying to bring him back from his world of rage and hate. He needs to understand that the police don't hate him and nobody is out to get him."

Nurse Bonnet was about to ask another question when the hospital PA system crackled, "Dr. Wong, Dr. Miso Wong. Please report to the admittance office."

Dr. Wong looked at his nurse he said, "Well that's me. It's probably another kid that took some drugs and is half out of his mind."

She answered, "Okay Doctor. Good luck down there and be safe."

Dr. Wong entered the elevator. He said, "Don't worry Nurse Bonnet. There will be two orderlies and at least one policeman there." The elevator door shut.

The next morning Dr. Wong arrived and found Nurse Bonnet and two orderlies waiting for him at O'Keefe's hospital room. He opened the door and walked in followed by them.

"Good morning Mr. O'Keefe, how are you doing this morning?"

Looking over to the doctor, O'Keefe answered, "I'm fine. How are you today?"

The doctor said, "I'm fine. But I'm not the one in the hospital. So let's talk about you."

Nurse Bonnet walked over to retrieve the metal cart with the shocking device on it. O'Keefe saw this and said, "Oh that won't be necessary nurse."

Dr. Wong asked, "Now who's the doctor here? Me or you patient O'Keefe?"

Nervously O'Keefe answered, "Well you are of course. But I feel just fine. And grounded."

Dr. Wong asked, "What do you think I mean when I say grounded?"

O'Keefe unsteadily answered, "I'm not sure. Maybe you want to know if I'm okay. "

"Mr. O'Keefe that is not what I mean. I am asking if you are with us. As in reality. Are you grounded in reality?" The doctor went on. "Why are you telling me that you are grounded when you don't know what I'm talking about?"

O'Keefe shook his head and mumbled, "I don't know. I thought maybe that's what you wanted to hear."

Dr. Wong said, "That's the problem Mr. O'Keefe. You saying what you think I want to hear. I need to hear the truth. And that's all."

Nurse Bonnet pushed the cart next to the bed and gave the power cord to one of the orderlies to go plug in. O'Keefe knew what that meant and started begging the doctor not to administer the shock treatment. He was talking 90 miles an hour and acting like he was crying. The doctor had put on the heavy rubber gloves and had the metal rods in his hands.

Looking at O'Keefe he asked, "Are you crying Mr. O'Keefe?"

O'Keefe answered with a look of terror on his face, "Yes I am crying and begging that you don't do this again to me."

Dr. Wong leaned over and put the metal rods on each side of O'Keefe's head and said, "But I don't see any tears. And with that he told nurse bonnet to flip the switch."

Chapter 7

Jack said goodbye to the last daytime regulars. It was around 3 o'clock. This is that brief time of the day when he is usually all alone. He wasn't making any money but he did enjoy the peace and quiet. While catching up on some paperwork, he heard the little bell ring. To his surprise it was Jolene. He asked, "What are you doing here? Your shift doesn't start for another two hours."

Jolene walked over and sat down on a barstool right by where Jack was working on some pub bills. "I think you know why I'm here. There are some things we need to talk about."

Jack said, "I still can't believe you figured all of this out."

Jolene said, "Jack, I've been giving you hints forever."

He said, "You have?"

"Yes, I have. Big ones." She continued. "How many times have I said to you? If anyone could do something, you can man."

Jack was truly stunned. "You were saying it right to my face and I didn't get it. Wow!"

Jolene went on, "And how many times have I said to you, I wish somebody could do something about someone."

Jack just shook his head in disbelief. "You were telling me this whole time that you knew who I was and I just didn't get it."

Jack started thinking, has anyone else dropped any subtle hints? He couldn't think of any. He thought, that's good.

Jolene continued, "The big guy that mugged me and also tried to strangle Officer Almond. His name is James Yellow Feather O'Keefe but guys in the department just refer to him as Dirty Feather."

Jack said, "Yes Jolene, I know who you are talking about. What about him?"

"Well, Alfie told me that he is going through shock treatment at the hospital. The doctor is one of the best at this sort of thing."

Jack said, "I hope it works. You know how I feel about anyone who wants to kill a cop."

Jolene said, "And you know how I feel about what you do. They both nodded in agreement."

Jack said, "I intend to keep a lookout for this guy whenever they let him out. I'm sure that is a good doctor, but they already let him out once before and he was worse than ever."

Jolene said, "Yes, you are correct Jack. But the doctor is well aware of that and is going to make real sure he is sane when they let him out again."

"I hope you are right," Jack answered. "While we are here by ourselves, I would like to ask you a question."

Jolene said, "Go ahead."

Jack asked, "I'm just curious. Have you been walking around at night on my tight ropes?"

The little bell above the door rang. They both looked up. It was Officer Alfie Alford.

Jolene said, "Honey, what are you doing here?"

Alfie said, "I was driving by and saw your car. Besides, I need to talk to Jack for a minute."

Jolene picked up her purse off of the bar and said, "Okay, you two can talk. I've got to run a few errands before my shift starts. I'll see you at 5 o'clock Jack." And she left.

Officer Alford turned to Jack and said, "I know that this may be none of my business, but I thought you and Firella were sort of seeing each other."

Jack answered, "I don't mind you asking. But the truth is we haven't been out on a date yet, but we talk."

Alfie asked, "The circus is in town and Jolene and I were thinking about going. We were wondering if you and Firella would like to go with us. You know, kind of a double date."

Jack said, "The circus? I thought that was for kids."

Alfie said, "Well, we just thought maybe going with us would make that first date a little easier. And the circus is not just for kids."

Jack looked down and said, "You are right about that making the first date easier. But who wants to go watch clowns with balloons for a couple of hours?"

Alfie said, "Jack it's not just clowns with balloons. There are lion tamers, trapeze artist and high wire acts. You know, tight rope walkers." Alfie went on. "Jolene was a gymnast for years and she likes that kind of stuff. What do you say Jack, it will be fun."

Jack answered, "Okay Alfie, I'll go. But I still have to ask Firella."

"Don't worry about that Jack," Alfie said. "Jolene has already asked Firella and she said yes."

Jack looked up and said, "You two have been busy."

Alfie laughed and said, "Yes we have." Alfie then added, "We are going this Sunday. Betsy will run the pub. Jolene already took care of that."

Jack said, "Okay, it looks like all I had to do was say yes. So let's go!"

Alfie shook his hand and left the pub. Jack went back to wiping down his bar and thought, *this could really be fun for Jolene and me to see a tight rope act. Too bad we won't be able to talk about it.*

Five o'clock rolled around and Jolene walked in followed by Betsy. They both put their purses away behind the bar and took their trays and went right to work. Customers were filing in.

Jolene came over to the bar with her first order. "Jack, I hope you didn't mind Alfie and me setting up this double date with Firella?"

Jack answered, "Of course not. Actually I thank you very much for doing that. And there's even a tight rope act. Well done Jolene."

Jolene put the last beer on her tray and said, "Thanks Jack. I wasn't sure if I was overstepping my bounds."

"No, no everything is fine," Jack said.

Chapter 8

Jack heard the crash of a table being tipped over and bottles and glasses breaking on the floor. He ran over to find two off duty cops fighting each other. Stepping in between the two to try and break it up, Jack caught a fist in the face. Falling into some chairs, Jack tried to catch his balance. Other off-duty cops immediately broke up the fight and separated the two. Jack was dazed and bleeding from his lip.

Chief Mike was standing in front of him. "Jack are you okay?" the chief asked as he was helping him up.

"Yes, I think so," Jack said as he rubbed his jaw.

Several officers righted the table and were putting the chairs back up. Jolene and Betsy swept up the broken glass and wiped down the table and chairs.

"Those two officers don't know it yet but they're paying for everything they broke," Chief Mike said. "Police are sometimes under a lot of stress and they just need to let off some pressure. But they can't do it here. They are supposed to act like brothers."

Jack was starting to feel a little better and said, "I used to fight with my real brother but that didn't mean I didn't love him. And one more thing, Chief. As the owner of Suzanna's Pub, I would like to ask that you go easy on them."

The chief answered, "I'll keep that in mind."

Jack could already feel his lip swelling and thought, *I think next time I'll let someone else break up a fight.*

The next morning Jack got to Suzanna's early to do some paperwork and let in Jose with a beer delivery. He was going through some bills when he heard the squeaky brakes of a delivery truck. He jumped up and unlocked the door then went back to his paperwork. The little bell on the door rang. Jack looked up to say hello to Jose. But it wasn't Jose. It was two big guys with some large boxes on dollies.

Jack said, "What's this, may I help you?"

"We have a delivery here for a table and chairs," said one of the delivery guys. "Where do you want it?"

Jack looked around and said, "I guess right here by the bar."

The two delivery men began opening boxes and assembling chairs. Jack was puzzled as to what was going on. The phone rang.

"Hello Jack. This is Chief Mike."

Jack responded, "Oh Hello Chief. What can I do for you?"

Chief Mike said, "Jack I'm calling you to see if you got a delivery today?"

Jack answered, "Well, yes I did. They are here now. What's this all about?"

The chief said, "You told me to take it easy on the two officers that were fighting in your Pub. I gave them a choice. They could buy you the best oak table and chairs they could find or be officially reprimanded. They chose option one."

Jack said, "I don't know what to say. They only broke a few glasses."

The chief said, "They did a lot more than that. They disrupted your business and you got punched in the mouth."

Jack thought for a second as he felt a swollen lip and said," I can't argue with you there."

Chief Mike said, "Listen Jack, I have to go now. Officers Morgan and Martinez are very sorry for the trouble they caused and hope you'll except this gift as their way of apologizing."

Jack said, "Of course." I'll let you go now. Thanks for the call."

Hanging up the phone Jack looked up to see the delivery men leaving with the empty boxes. "Thanks guy," he said as the little bell rang and the door shut.

Jose pulled up and started unloading beer cases. Looking over at the new table, he was very impressed with this beauty. The four heavy oak chairs had black leather seats and backs. The table was round with a heavy oak stand under the middle. It had a very shiny finish.

Jack thought *this fancy table makes all the rest look bad. I think I'm going to keep it here up front since this is where we all like to sit after we lock the door behind the last customer.* Jack sat in one of the new chairs and thought, *this is more comfortable than my chairs in my apartment.*

Looking up at the clock it was almost time to open. He cleared all of the paperwork off of the bar. The phone rang again. It was Firella.

"Hey Jack are you getting excited about tomorrow night?"

Jack sort of asked, "Tomorrow night?"

Firella said in a louder voice, "Yes tomorrow night. Did you forget about us going to the circus with Jolene and Alfie?"

Jack quickly said, "Of course not. How can I forget that? I've just had my mind on this business. We can talk more later. My daytime regulars are waiting outside for me to open the door."

Firella said before hanging up, "Okay great! I can't remember the last time I went to the circus. We will have fun. Bye for now."

Jose stopped at the bar after delivering the last beer cases. Jack gave him an ice cold bottle of water.

Jose said, "That's a fancy table. I better get going to my next stop."

Jack waved goodbye to him. He thought about his not remembering the double date to the circus. Firella didn't seem upset. He was happy about that. And went back to taking care of his customers.

Chapter 9

The next day late in the afternoon Jack was getting ready to go to the pub to meet everyone for the double date. Looking in the mirror he wondered how he should to dress to go to the circus. He decided to dress the same way he would any other date.

Driving a few blocks to his pub, he was wondering how Dirty Feather was doing. *That Dr. Wong is supposed to be good. I guess we will find out someday. But if Dirty Feather has any crazy ideas about killing cops, the Can Man will deal with him.*

Back at the mental hospital, Nurse Bonnet was walking with Dr. Wong on their way to O'Keefe's room.

She asked, "Doctor. Do you think O'Keefe is getting better?"

He responded, "Well, Nurse Bonnet, it is hard to tell. The mind is a mysterious thing. All we can do is make evaluations."

She asked, "And what's the best way to evaluate?"

He said, "I ask him questions. Preferably questions that will raise emotions. Then see how he answers. What I'm trying to do is get to the bottom of his source of rage and stop it. If I can't stop it he will either end up in prison or dead."

Walking into the room the doctor said hello to patient O'Keefe. "How are you doing today Mr. O'Keefe?"

"Oh I'm just fine," He answered.

The doctor asked him, "A little bird told me that you referred to Judge Dinkle as Dinky Dinkle. Is that true?"

O'Keefe answered, "Well, yes I did call him that one time. He is really short and I was upset at the time."

Dr. Wong asked, "Do you still think of him as Dinky Dinkle?"

O'Keefe looked up at the doctor and said, "Oh no. I have completely changed since then. I believe he is doing a tough job and is a good man."

Dr. Wong said, "Mr. O'Keefe, I like what you just said." He made a note on his clipboard. Looking back up at O'Keefe, Dr. Wong asked, "Did you know that some of the police referred to you as Dirty Feather instead of Yellow Feather?"

"Yes I know," said O'Keefe. "When they were locking me up and they knew I attacked that lady cop, they were pretty upset with me. They called me Dirty Feather as they shoved me into that cell."

Dr. Wong asked, "How do you feel about these police officers now?"

O'Keefe said, "I think they also have a tough job and don't get the credit they deserve."

Dr. Wong nodded his head. "Very good, Mr. O'Keefe. I like your response." Dr. Wong made another note on his clipboard. He looked up at O'Keefe. "I just have one more question. Do you still want to kill Officer Almond?"

Answering O'Keefe said, "Of course not. I feel really terrible about that and I wish I could tell her how sorry I am."

Dr. Wong smiled and spoke as he jotted down another note. "Mr. O'Keefe, I truly believe you are getting better. You gave the answers I was looking for on every question. I'm telling you this because I think you need to know that you are getting better."

O'Keefe said, "Thank you for telling me."

"But I also know that you have given me answers saying what you think I want to hear," Dr. Wong said. "And I'm going to administer another round of shock treatment."

To the doctors amazement O'Keefe said, "Okay. Whatever you think is best."

Dr. Wong placed the metal rods on either side of O'Keefe's head, "This will be your last shock treatment Mr. O'Keefe."

"Thank you doctor. Proceed."

Chapter 10

As the electricity was going through O'Keefe's head, Jack was walking into a giant circus tent with Firella. She was clinging to his arm like an excited little girl. They stopped to get popcorn, cotton candy and sodas. Alfie lead the way into the huge arena. They all sat down with Jack sitting between the girls. They were so happy to be there.

Firella leaned over to Jack and said, "This is so cool. And they really do have three big rings down there." The noise was very loud so she was having to shout. "I just don't know how this could get any more exciting Jack."

Firella felt a tap on her shoulder. Turning around, she looked up and saw a man standing there wearing a very bright white and red suit with coattails. He had a black top hat and cane.

The man said, "Hello there Madame. My name is Mr. French. I am the Ringmaster of the circus. I noticed your beautiful red hair and was wondering if you would give us the honor of riding on top of our Fairytale float? It is a carriage in the shape of a giant pumpkin and will be drawn by six white horses."

"Are you kidding me? I would love to ride on top of your float."

The Ringmaster took her hand and told everyone, "She will be back after her ride around the arena floor."

Jack turned to Jolene and Alfie and said, "Can you believe this? Firella is going to be a part of the circus." They all high-fived each other.

The high powered spot lights came on and lit up Mr. French. He said in a booming voice, "Ladies and gentlemen. Welcome to the biggest and best circus on earth."

The huge crowd roared and applauded.

"Please direct your attention over here." He pointed his cane to a large colorful curtain. Out came a huge elephant followed by smaller elephants each holding the tale of the elephant in front of them. A brightly painted small car followed. And yes it was packed with clowns. They all piled out and danced and carried on behind the elephants.

Jack spotted the first white horses coming out. Behind those six white horses was a large, beautiful sparkling pumpkin shaped carriage. And on top was none other than Firella. She was wearing a princess dress, and smiling and waving as she went around the arena.

Mr. French said, "Everyone please give a big round of applause to Firella, our Fairy Tale Princess."

The floodlights made Firella's red hair light up. The place went nuts.

Later, Firella return to her seat. She sat down and said, "Jack, I think I'm dreaming."

Jack laughed. "Firella, you are not dreaming."

Jolene said, "You are not dreaming. You really were riding on top of a giant pumpkin carriage pulled by six white horses."

Jack pointed Firella's attention the other way. There stood Mr. French.

Mr. French said, "Firella you were fantastic and the crowd loved you. As a token of our appreciation here at the circus we would like to give you the tiara you were wearing down there."

Firella was shocked. "Are you kidding me? This has got to be a dream. I get to keep the tiara?"

Mr. French said, "Yes, it's yours," He handed her the tiara and said, "Thank you, Firella for being our fairy princess. I have to get back down to the arena floor, now. Coming up next is the high wire act followed by the lion tamers. You're going to love this."

Firella put the tiara on her head and asked Jack, "How do I look?"

He said, "You look like a real princess."

Jolene said "You are not dreaming. But this is just like a dream."

About then they heard the booming voice of Mr. French. "Ladies and gentlemen, please direct your attention to the high wire act." He pointed his cane up to the tight ropes. All of the performers were wearing colorful tights. The first one walked out with a long balancing pole.

Jolene leaned over and whispered to Jack, "Anybody can do that with the pole. They should try it with no pole."

Jack felt a tug on his shirt. It was Firella and she asked, "Jack, what is Jolene talking about?"

Jack was quickly thinking, *I can't just tell her that I am the Can Man and Jolene sometimes walks on my tight ropes.* After a small pause Jack said, "Firella, you may not know this but Jolene was a gymnast growing up and can tight rope walk herself. She was just commenting that she does it without the use of a pole."

Firella looked at Jolene and said, "Wow! I didn't know you could do that. I always thought you were in great shape and took good care of yourself but I didn't realize you could tight rope."

Jolene said, "Thanks Firella. I do like to stay in shape but I don't really do all that stuff anymore."

After the lion tamer act finished Jack leaned over and said to Alfie, "If we leave now we will miss the crush of everyone else leaving at once."

Alfie looked at Jolene and said, "What do you think Jolene?"

She said, "Sounds good to me."

Jack turned to Firella and asked, "How about you?"

Firella answered, "Ditto."

They all got up and made their way out to the parking lot and returned to the pub. It was closed and dark inside. However, the parking lot was well lit.

Jolene said," Jack I'm so glad you got those lights installed."

He answered, "Me too."

Jolene said, "Thanks for driving."

Jack said, "Thank you and Alfie for setting all of this up."

Alfie and Jack shook hands. Firella and Jolene hugged.

After they drove off, Jack said to Firella, "Let me walk you to your car."

She said, "Jack, I was thinking, your parking lot is well lit and has security cameras, right?"

Jack said "Yes it does."

She went on, "Well, I was thinking I could just leave my car here overnight and just stay at your place. Would that be okay with you?"

Jack looked at the ground and said, "Well, let me think about that ... I'm just kidding. Of course you can come over."

Firella said, "I just have one request."

"Okay, what's that?"

She said, "All I ask is that you don't ask me to take off this tiara." They both laughed and got in his car.

Chapter 11

The next morning Chief Mike was sitting at his desk doing some paperwork when the phone rang. "Hello, this is Chief Mike. How can I help you?

The voice answered, "Hello Chief. This is Dr. Wong at the county mental hospital."

The Chief said, "Oh yes Dr. Wong. I heard you were treating O'Keefe. How's it coming along? How's he doing?"

Dr. Wong said, "Well, that's actually why I am calling. He has been doing very well but I am still evaluating him. Which brings me as to why am calling you."

Chief Mike said, "You are calling me about evaluating him? How can I help?"

The doctor went on, "I have been running numerous test on him. He apparently was released before from the hospital and was worse than ever. Now he is making vast improvements but I need to run one more test on him. And this is where you come in."

The Chief was really curious now as to how he could help the doctor test O'Keefe. "Okay Doc. How can I help with that?"

Dr. Wong responded. "I want O'Keefe to face the officer he attacked as well as lots of other police officers. I want to see how he reacts and what he says.

Chief Mike said, "I think that is a great test. However, I need to talk to Officer Almond first. Can I call you back tomorrow?"

Dr. Wong said, "Of course. Thank you for your help. I just hope Officer Almond is willing to face her attacker and assist me in evaluating Mr. O'Keefe."

Chief Mike said, "I'll give you a call tomorrow and tell you what she said. Goodbye."

Firella and Sasha were working the school zone again looking for speeders when the car radio crackled. "Chief Mike would like Officer Almond to see him after your shift is over."

Firella picked up the mic and said, "Roger that."

Sasha asked, "What's that all about?"

Firella answered, "I don't know. I guess I'll find out later."

Back at Susana's Pub the bar phone rang.

Jack walked over and picked it up and said, "Hello. Susanna's Pub. How can I help you?"

The voice said, "Hello Jack. This is Chief Mike calling from the station. I was wondering if you have a minute. I would like to run something by you."

Jack said, "Of course, what's up?"

The Chief said, "I just got off the phone with Dr. Wong from the county mental hospital. He has asked me if I would be willing to help him evaluate O'Keefe."

Jack said after a pause," O'Keefe. He wants you to help? How are you going to do that?"

The Chief said, "Well, I was thinking you could help me. "

Jack was more confused than ever now. "So let me get this straight. Dr. Wong wants you to help him evaluate O'Keefe and I am somehow a part of this? Is that right?"

Chief Mike said, "Yes. Let me explain. The doctor would like O'Keefe to face Firella. And he also wants him to face lots of other officers. He needs to see his reactions, what he says and how he responds to the whole meeting."

Jack said, "Let me guess. Do you want to have it here at Suzanna's Pub?"

Chief Mike said, "Correct. We already have lots of off-duty law-enforcement there and they will give Firella some comfort. What do you say Jack?"

Jack said, "Its okay with me. But have you talked to Firella yet?"

The chief said, "Not yet. She's coming to see me after her shift ends."

Jack said, "Okay. Just let me know when you want to have it here. "

The chief said, "That's great Jack. Thanks for helping me out on this."

Jack said, "Glad I can help. Talk to you later."

Jack hung up the phone. He started thinking, what is the upside to this? He thought, *well, I guess if it helps Dr. Wong, that's good. And I guess if it helps O'Keefe that's good. But on the downside if O'Keefe has a relapse and goes nuts with all of those cops there, well who knows what could happen.*

Chapter 12

The next morning Jack was at his pub early and the phone rang. Before he answered he had a feeling it was the chief. "Hello, Susanna's Pub. How may I help you?"

"Hi Jack, its Chief Mike. I am calling you to let you know that I talked with Officer Almond and she has agreed to a meeting with O'Keefe. If it's okay with you I would like to do it tonight at your pub."

Jack said, "Okay with me Chief. It's probably best to get it over with. Sooner rather than later."

The chief said, "I agree. Dr. Wong will be bringing O'Keefe over around 6 o'clock tonight."

Jack said, "Okay. I'll see everyone then."

Looking up at the wall clock, Jack thought, *this is either going to be a good thing or a nightmare. Everyone in that room is going to be ready to protect Firella if things go south.*

Late that afternoon lots of off-duty cops started filing in. More than usual. And there were some that were in uniform. They were drinking bottled water. Jack already knew that Chief Mike wasn't taking any chances. He had his men there to handle any problems. Firella came in and sat at the end of the bar.

Jack walked over and asked, "Are you okay? Are you ready for this?"

She said, "I am ready. Sometimes in life you have to face your fear head on. And I refuse to let fear rule my life."

Jack said, "Me and every cop in here has your back."

She said, "Thanks Jack. Also, all I want right now is a bottle of water."

Jack said, "I'll be right back."

Sasha came in and sat down next to Firella.

Everyone seem to be glancing up at the clock and for the pub to be that full, he hadn't heard one bit of laughter. On cue, the whole room went silent. And in walked none other than James Yellow Feather O'Keefe followed by Dr. Wong and two orderlies in their white jackets. The orderlies stayed at the front door. Dr. Wong and O'Keefe walked up to the bar. Dr. Wong shook Jack's hand and thanked him for allowing this evaluation to take place at his pub. He turned to Chief Mike who was sitting at the bar and thanked him for setting this up.

Dr. Wong said in a loud voice, "May I have your attention please. My name is Dr. Wong and I am one of the lead doctors at the county mental hospital. Mr. Warren has been kind enough to allow me to use his pub to do an evaluation on patient O'Keefe here. He motioned to O'Keefe. As many of you know Mr. O'Keefe was released from the hospital with hatred in his heart for the police. He tried to kill Officer Almond. The judge believed that Mr. O'Keefe deserved one more chance at the hospital. I took it upon myself to take care of this case. Mr. O'Keefe has been the subject of many test procedures. I now believe he is nearing his release from the hospital. But before I sign off on his release I wanted to run one last test. Officer Firella Almond has agreed to this test."

Dr. Wong walked over to Firella. "Are you ready?"

Firella said, "Yes I am."

Dr. Wong said, "Ask him anything you want. Also feel free to tell him anything you want. I need to see how he reacts."

She said, "Okay. Let's do this."

While walking over to O'Keefe, Dr. Wong motioned for the two orderlies to come in a little closer. Dr. Wong said to O'Keefe, "This is officer Firella Almond. Do you remember that you tried to strangle her to death? Just for being a police officer. Do you remember?"

O'Keefe cleared his throat and said, "I don't remember your face. I just remember attacking a police officer. I wasn't myself back then and I had a lot of anger. And I'm telling you now that

I am so sorry for that day. It wasn't against you personally. I hope you will forgive me."

Firella thought for a moment. "Mr. O'Keefe. Dr. Wong said that you are much, much better now and I want to believe him." Then she did something no one expected. She walked right up to O'Keefe. She looked him right in the eyes and said, "If you want to kill me now is the time. I'm right here. You could snap my neck before anyone could reach you."

Every cop in there stood up, ready to pounce if this didn't go well. Jack thought this is a little on the dangerous side, moving closer from behind the bar.

O'Keefe said, "No, I don't want to kill you or anyone else. I wish only good and safe things ahead for you and your fellow officers. I know this might sound funny, but I hope someday I can help you out."

Dr. Wong stepped in and said, "Well, Mr. O'Keefe, Officer Almond. Thank you for helping with this evaluation. I have one final question."

Firella returned to her barstool.

Sasha said to her, "That was good although you scared the heck out of all of us."

Firella said, "Sorry, but for me I had to face my fear."

Sasha said, "Well you did, literally."

Dr. Wong said to everyone, "If you think patient O'Keefe is ready and fit to be released from the hospital, please raise your hand."

Nobody moved at first. Everyone looked over at Firella. She saw them looking at her. She looked at O'Keefe and raised her hand high. All of the other officers followed suit and raise their hands.

Dr. Wong said to everyone, "Thank you for being here for this evaluation."

He turned to O'Keefe and said, "Mr. O'Keefe, I believe you are cured and ready to be a good citizen. So I am here by officially releasing you from the hospital."

O'Keefe started to get a little misty eyed and said, "I don't know what to say except thank you so much for helping me."

Dr. Wong shook his hand and said, "You are welcome."

One of the orderlies brought over a suitcase and handed it to the doctor. Reaching into his pocket, Dr. Wong pulled out a brown envelope and said to O'Keefe, "Here is a suitcase with your belongings and here is the envelope with some money to help you get started on your new life."

O'Keefe said, "Thank you so much. And when you see Nurse Bonnet tell her thank you for me."

"Will do," said the doctor.

Jack walked over and asked Firella, "How are you doing?"

She said, "I'm actually doing just fine. As a matter of fact I feel like a big burden has been lifted off of me."

Jack said, "That's great."

Firella said, "Jack, I was wondering if I could stay again at your place tonight?"

Jack of course had to pretend that he had to think about it. Then answered, "Well I guess that would be okay. But there's just one problem."

Firella looked at him and said, "There's a problem? I really wanted to stay over tonight."

Jack said, "Of course you can stay over but the problem is you don't have your tiara."

Firella laughed and said, "Oh yes I do. It's in my car."

They both laughed. Firella got up close to Jacks ear and whispered, "If anyone can cheer up a girl, you can...man."

Made in the USA
Monee, IL
25 September 2020

42681115R00056